Belle

A Novella

Sam Francis O'Doherty

BELLE

ISBN 978-1-4092-5100-2

© 2008 Sam Francis O'Doherty

Dedicated to anybody who
wonders why,
and anybody who
needs a reason to try.

Prelude

The clearing of the fog,
In the forest of the mind,
In a cloud of lustful mercy,
A busy calm, one can find.
The changing of a season,
Would be nothing without emotion,
But the changing of emotion,
Is dead, but to the soul.

It was a cliché, they knew that.

All of them, sitting there, on the wooden plank, the bark encrusted with years of vomit, the occasional blood spill and the melancholy smell of mildew. Nothing was quite as incredible for the group, as the effect that the setting had on their mood.

It was unprecedented that the six of them were brought together with the common aim of finding their common ground. The ground between the gunfire, and the tellings-off that went with it, from the bankruptcy and the city jobs and from the hazy mellowing of Thursday night, by the bigger of the two oak trees, where smoking was always permitted.

The moon. A blurry reflection of a drunk-man's eyeball, all silence and movement.

Silent movement.

Like the footfalls that were dominating the realm of the beetle. An evanescence of time, vacuum-packed into a matchbox-sized portion. Illegality never bothered Belle; just the thought that she might be found out.

A reasonable fear, they all assumed.

Assumption had never really gotten them anywhere that they wanted to be.

Belle threw the cigarette butt on the floor. It hissed as it hit the moist leaves of the clearing. Her red dress was being dirtied by the implicitly dank properties of the plank, which was sagging under her minimal weight; the bolts that held it to the two stumps had rusted, and had rouged the bark along with the alloy.

It wasn't her favourite dress, anyway.

No, her favourite dress was long gone. A memory along with all the others: not necessarily as debauched, she had to admit, but memorable nonetheless.

A swig of cheap cider met Belle's lips, the acidic properties seemingly tangible in the air, as they swept up her nostrils, and then down her already raw throat; nauseated apples were nauseating apples, she decided, as she put the can down and swore never to drink again.

Three minutes passed, her hands beginning to feel tense under the stresses that the environment was forcing them to endure; the bitter cold that could only be found in secret clearings, or in novels, or in the imagination. Only the first was true: it was a place of secrecy.

Belle broke another promise. Skipping the lifetime of abstinence, she lifted the can to her lips, and swigged at the once fruity mixture of sharpness: seawater without salt, or needles with an apple tainted point. Cider never agreed with her. The chemicals in her brain mistrusted the stories from her conscious thought, reassuring them that it was a low alcohol consumption, and decided instead to listen to her empty stomach, and her blood's need to gather it's contents from somewhere.

As she felt the first pangs of intoxication, she realised that her dress was no longer hiding the bruises.

Or that her blonde hair was no longer hiding her eyes. Or that nothing was hiding her from the other five.

Nearest to her, joint in hand as always, Abigail remained calm as plumes of her obliging smoke rushed up to meet her bleached hair, which was propped up against the smaller of the two trees. Her body was relaxed; her arms and legs were warm, despite winter's lordship over the heat of the sun.

Belle had known her for nearly a year, yet still used Abigail's full name, not Abby, or Abs. It was never as easy for monosyllabically named children to understand the concept of abbreviation, or shortening. It had, though, been a long time since Belle was a monosyllabic child.

She lit another cigarette.

Took another swig of cider.

Ten years, since she dropped out of Uni. Ten years since she both thought she knew enough, and knew she didn't think enough. Ten years since she was a monosyllabic child.

With a quick glance back at Abigail, and the two trees, and the smoke, Belle shifted her shoeless feet to cross each other, dragged across the sodden ground, still shining from the latest bout of December's perspiration. Her attempts to manoeuvre away from the breeze didn't help her to avoid the winter – the cider did that for her. She sat and contemplated the birthday landmark coming towards her, hoping that a sense of satisfaction with her achievements would manage to find her, and pin her down, for the first time in the thirty-year quest.

Beyond the glance, beyond Abigail and the two trees, the larger of the oak's being nearer to the overgrowth – the hedged border of the clearing – the smaller of the two being nearer Belle and the rust-bolted bench – a suit was stood, black, accented by the white shirt underneath, hanging from male flesh, tight enough to show contour, loose enough to hide flab.

The black tie finished the funeral attire, with its pointed finish stopping neatly just below the shirt's lowest button, and leading up to Jack's neck. Tightly noosed, but in the most articulate fashion.

Jack was, as his name often gave away; male. Although, he would flagrantly disregard such insults with a wave of his hand, or a wry smile, or a sarcastic comment to outwardly move on conversation, and inwardly to further depreciate his inverted ego.

Masculinity was relative to him, but paramount to his father. The hands at the ends of the suit's sleeves, however, would never have suited the old bastard; they weren't calloused from labour, or crinkled from late nights defending masculine pride outside a pub.

Jacks hands were certainly tied; but with nothing as forgiving as handcuffs.

Belle turned again from her seat, not wanting to have to get up, and looked him in the eye. His non-responsive manner was fitting, he never really said much, and in the mood that he had been in recently, nobody had really heard much from him at all. The occasional text message; but that was only on account of his fear of being totally forgotten being a stronger impulse than that of his fear of becoming dependent on anything.

The three of them were still silent, except for the occasional movement of Belle's feet, her smooth legs spanning down to the muddy soles that occasionally tapped out a rhythm on the earth stage beneath her.

Still, due to a combination of nonchalance, the cold and an introduction of the heart-warming, soul-destroying effects of alcohol, she was unaware that the shortness of the red dress had revealed to any vigilant eyes, browny-blue patches. Bruises. Splodges of darkness underneath the skin, proof of the frailty of the human body.

Opposing the three figures, spread out sporadically, more jam than butter, was another scene; another branch of the same tree, the other three of the six, the other half. As was the nature of nature, the most unnatural formations seemed to intersperse themselves on occasion into the rugged notoriety of panoramic views. Like crop circles on a massive and temporal scale.

The clearing was one of those lucid points, where time walked the perimeter, her warrior instinct quelled by the takeover of stillness. Calm was an unnerving presence, especially when it came in the deviant form of five figurines and Belle.

Following the curvature of the clearing, behind Belle, opposite Abigail, slumped cross-legged, was the ever-resourceful Shona. Red hair from crown, down her back, to drift off into thinner, wavier strands of the firebrand's fire brand, stopping just in time for her jeans to start.

Shona was the least quiet of the six, oftentimes the mouthpiece. Her voice was cutting, but in the paper way, more than the knife. With no effort, her vocal chords could fill a room, turn its entire heads, and make them smile.

It was the Irish in her.

The electricity of her voice was powered by the shocking blue of her eyes, enhanced by the elfin curvature of her nose. Neat features. Yes; Shona was a neat package. *Was* a neat package.

Belle took a sip of the cider. Her eyes blinked. Then blinked again. The can was dead. Belle has murdered it, taken all that was good from it, and left the shell. A process that she was resigning herself to becoming accustomed to. With a sudden thrust of her arm, the can flew, and she watched it. The can moved off, spittle from the residual thimbleful amount was left jumping overboard in an attempt to stay in the clearing and not touch the outside world, not touch the real world; Belle pondered this and that, turning ideas over in her head.

With a sort of jadedly docile liveliness, she lifted herself off of the rust-bolted bench, and sunk to her knees. She turned, surveying all that was before her. Sometimes it seemed to her that the clearing was her kingdom, her own personal domain. Nothing that haunted anybody could permeate the intangible, shadowy barriers that separated her and her thoughts from the outside

Belle's arms rose, and she leant forward, her elbows resting on the centre of the bench; a mathematically equal distance from both side, from both rusty bolts, she noted, as she gave her head a shake, moving her wild blonde hair away from her face. The soles of her feet now faced up to the sky, doing a chameleon impression; if it wasn't for the toned, pale legs that they were attached to, they could pass for a part of the dead-leaf carpeting.

Jack's face contorted slightly, as if he was uncomfortable momentarily, but he soon got over it, moving back into position. He was looking down at Shona, still cross-legged, still red-headed, as the light began to change. The moon blinked as a cloud passed overhead.

Then the pallid song of the moonlight continued to play through the muted atmosphere. Jack's gaze was not on Shona, but on the figure behind her. He was like Jack in so much as they were both male, but he was unlike Jack in so much as he was a man. There would always be differences between them that maybe neither of them acknowledged socially and, at this stage, neither of them particularly needed to.

Jack stared with compassionate disclosure at Max, who simply returned the look with a peaceful sense of acceptance. Of the two, the latter was far happier with the situation, whether it was expected or not. He found it hard to care.

Max had two hands, but only one was free. The other was enveloped awkwardly in the firm grip of the short, the fat, and the ugly. Sandra. As Belle surveyed the clearing, like she had been doing for the ten seconds since she let the cider can fly away, she noticed how contrasting Max' slender – maybe too slender – figure looked, compared with Sandra's plump – definitely too plump – outer layer.

Belle played with her hair, running her fingernails through it, scratching her scalp, feeling the effects of the alcohol toying with her impulses, sending electricity through her body, numbing her skin. Only her nose was still cold. The moon looked down on the clearing, its infinite angles, the six internal components well assembled. There was more silence, but it began to grow thick. The distant assumption that there was noise elsewhere halted like a train in the dark, the panicked passengers scrambling in the same way that dreams had a tendency to do in the dark, alone, without interruption.

It was only then that Belle noticed, from the positioning of the six, by the roaring silence around them, the persistent sense of composure, the way her heart was fighting; a maggot in hot acid writhing around inside of her, trying to break through her ribcage, that they seemed to be waiting.

In a way, that was true.

CHAPTER I

Lies & Hope

Capturing the imagination and capturing the heart were two very different things; Abigail had learnt that at an early age. For someone capable of reaching such philosophical heights, she had often questioned why it was she never seemed to be able to figure out which junction to leave at. The motorway spanned on, and her foot – to her great annoyance – stayed stuck on the accelerator.

Every week, the same mistake, and every week, her internal monologue was filled with the expletives that would make a bishop die.

There it was.

With a particularly unholy *Bollocks!* she swerved the car to one side, the tyres complained as they did every week, and she, as usual, ignored them. Roundabout. Third exit. Straight ahead. Left.

As the roads narrowed, she felt a sense of direction return to her, and senses of reassurance and purpose came with it like the emotional sheep that they were. The wheels of the little red car once again complained, as she pulled into his driveway. The gravel underneath crunched. The tired tyres had an overtly conspicuous manner, as if they wanted the attention that was about to be lavished on their controller. Abigail wrenched on the handbrake, as if to re-assert her mastery over the seemingly jealous tyres.

What her tyres, or the rest of the world, thought of her was irrelevant. She was minutes away from being with him. She wanted to avoid the overused, over-poetic descriptions of love – maybe that was why she didn't keep a diary.

Final checks: lips reddened up, eyes sharpened up, boobs pushed up.

She was ready.

In an automatic motion, she flung open the door, swung her legs round. Semi-opaque tights, red leather stilettos, little black dress. Tall, slim, bleach-blonde. She began to glide over the gravel, slamming the door behind her, locking the car didn't even cross her mind. Nothing, particularly, crossed her mind.

The doorbell rang.

The seven heartbeats that it took for him to get to the door were longer than the seven last week, but no time compared to the millions that thumped their way out in the six days in between. The door opened. Confident smile. Sexy smile. Genuine smile. She didn't notice his failed efforts to look at her face before her breasts, as his arms were on their way around her before she had time to notice anything more than the blur that everything was becoming. A sweet blur, the one that she craved.

Talking of cravings.

She smelt the cannabis on his shirt. There was a time that he would have changed after work before succumbing to illicit lure, but he decided that Wilde was right, and they could both resist anything but temptation. Their bodies embraced, and the whiteness enveloped them both. A gentle balm soaked into their skin; a mixture of omitted affection being made up for, the ecstasy of amorous tactility and raw compulsion.

Another seven heartbeats passed, but this time they were not from two hungry hearts, but two satisfied hearts, dancing in restful conversation.

The door slammed, unbeknown to them, betwixt in a passionate flurry, moving through the house, through the lounge door, the peach carpet becoming decoratively clothed, as the two treated the stairs like a pretend obstacle, themselves losing clothes. In another philosophical moment, in the time it took her to blink, Abigail stole a certain admiration for the way in which creatures of such renowned civilisation as people resorted to, and lavished in, moments of such pure animal passion.

The boundaries of reality could be warped. Icarus tried it with the sun and got burned. Man is constantly trying it with every step, sometimes losing and sometimes just not winning. Abigail was pushing every boundary, nominally losing her singularity, her individuality, willingly giving herself to him.

As the moments became heated, time's ability to keep the clock ticking at a steady pace was forgotten, then sun's ability to illuminate was relinquished; both boundless time and moonlight became the audience for fervour.

All good performances come to an end.

There was no applause, just a mutually respective repose.

The bed was all arms and legs, as it became a ship and sailed off into the night, joining the rest of Abigail's reality in a rhythmically succinct realm of idealistic romances, and dreams that came true. Along with consciousness, higher philosophical questions took a hiatus for the hours that she was asleep, but as she stepped into the reception area between awake and asleep, she was reassured to notice the monochrome of the place; for the first time, her life was more colourful than her dreams.

It never started first time. Ever. In absolute defiance, the engine would not turn over, and in absolute desperation, Abigail kept trying.

No, no, no.

It was useless, she was sure, but as her mother would tell her, *try, try, and try again.*

Not only was it five o'clock in the morning, but somehow, in nocturnal engrossment, her tights had become lone agents, and hidden from her, making the morning air particularly fresh and the winter breeze particularly acute.

No, no, no.

She gripped the steering wheel in the vain hope that she could somehow coerce the car into starting. The torture was totally ineffective. In another blink of philosophical lucidity, Abigail was amused at how one could become so completely devoted to the animal instinct hours before, then so suddenly and coldly crash land back to the steely reality of industrial man, and have the romantic notion of unending time cut short by the lack of emotion in that which humans relied on.

But the philosophy lecture was shelved as her groans of annoyance were replaced by the lethargic wheezing of her car's engine. It was as if the bolts, welded metal and oil had accepted her philosophical plea that they were not dictated to by emotion or reason, and in a moment of self-realisation, decided to make something happen.

Yes, yes, yes.

Reverse. First. Accelerate.

Don't look back.

Abigail looked back defiantly.

The pangs had started already, maybe she was weak, maybe she was idealistic. Probably both. But, she thought she was happy. Change gear. Maybe she was becoming too attached; had the days of failing marriage, leading to a fully fledged failed marriage not taught her anything? This was different; this wasn't the soap opera that her ex was. This was the drama with deadly romantic scenes interspersed. The sort of thing that made the middle-aged teary. She turned the radio on. Of course, the universe being what it is, the radio did nothing for Abigail's mood, supplied no up tempo number to distract her momentarily, but instead a somber ballad.

It was quaint really.

As a sympathetic teardrop threatened to leap off of her eyelid, she decided she was indeed in love with him, and he was indeed in love with her.

Jack could hardly be expected to be the hero.

She was in love with him.

Not the end of the world, he had dealt with worse. *Toughen up, boy.* His father's voice was, as usual, echoing around in the back of his head somewhere. Saying nothing in particular. Why was she in love with him?

He didn't have time to care. There were more pressing matters at hand. Moreover, there was the single pressing issue of how to explain the well-worn tights behind the sofa to his boyfriend

In her secret life, she was a poem being read by some divine voice. A story recounted to children of the future as a morality lesson, in some encrypted formation that would be more moving to the teacher than the student. Abigail's finality was not succinct, and her superstitious nature dissuaded her from making moves towards putting pen to paper.

The journey back home was as unrivalled in excitement as she had grown accustomed to. Of course, her devotion to Prince Charming was something to keep her mind busy with. Thinking about him was like constantly solving the world's most difficult equation for the first time.

Even paperwork, the scourge of the material world, seemed more bearable.

In one of her many philosophical moments of the day – for which she thought she would be better publicised for, yet never had the courage to voice – she questioned when she was going to step off and realise that she was on a train to nowhere. Then she decided it probably didn't matter, that all trains went to the same eventual destination, and continued looking down at the shipment forms.

For an educated girl she had done surprisingly poorly for herself.

Public schooled. Decent university graduate. Met Marcus at 21. Married Marcus at 21. First went into hospital because of Marcus at 21. He loved her. Yes. Totally devoted.

It did not take an ounce of her philosophical potential to see that he was taking advantage of her for her body, and her parents for their money. The most unsavoury of characters are often the sweetest. Trust was something that came easily between the two of them. He was her zenith; there was nothing to her life after him. He hurt her because he loved her; that was just how it was. Her friends did not need to understand – none of them were married, none of them had any experience, she was clearly the better person. The better woman. Abigail hated the fact that for three years, she was close to believing that bullshit.

She tore herself away; packed two bags, one red, one black, and loaded the car which, of course, refused to start at first. No, no, no. The theatre went on, the car felt appreciated, the car started.

Abigail found freedom to be a terrifying thing. Maybe that was at the route of everything; she had been pampered from childhood by her parents, they had money enough to pay social bullets to dissolve; enough money even to pay the gunmen to look elsewhere. Then as the institutionalisation ended, the doors were opened for her – unfortunately, before she set foot outside, in stepped Marcus with his expensive aftershave and polished teeth. Charm, cashmere and qualifications.

The ideal husband. The idealistic husband.

Idealism was a dirty path and Abigail always had dirty shoes.

One punch. Nose.

Two punches. Ribs.

Three punches. Ribs.

Four and five punches. Ribs and nose.

The familiar feel of sensual drowsiness leapt onto Jack's back, his mouth falling open to try his normal plea for forgiveness, but the attempt was thwarted by a surge of hot, bittersweet blood. Not quite enough force to be projectile, too much to be a dribble.

With a cough that his father considered pathetic, the glutinous liquid marred his white shirt with an impressively destructive shade of red. He was partially aware that paternal affection had swiped him round the mouth once more, but his brain was far too preoccupied with the process of neutralising the pain.

The brain was, after all, one of the few friends that one had in unnatural situations; it was only when that started to fail that the cause started to become distant.

Jack was still caringly hugged by his suit as he dropped. His right knee was the pathfinder, leading by example for the rest of his body, landing in a part-petroleum puddle. His suit, although not impressed with being dipped in oil, was a loyal friend, and kept Jack as warm as it could for the hours between dark and light, when the minimal heat of the morning sun offered a helping hand.

His father would not have it. No son of his would be *one of them*. No son of his would *let the family down*. Apparently, Jack's mother would *turn in her grave*. His son was supposed to be *a real man*.

It didn't really matter how many omnipotent or stereotypical phrases his father ensured were thrown in, the fact was a fact. Unfortunately the possibility that there was another side to the situation, failed to register. An explanation would just result in *effing ungrateful* and *mixed up*.

Jack had recounted the entire situation a thousand times in his head. Should he not have told the man that was once his dad, the truth? It was after that day, after that truth, that he was no longer *dad* or a friend. He was a stranger. A stranger that Jack missed. That day was a pivot, a chapter in the depressiveness of the Russian novel that his life seemed to have become. Maybe he wasn't as similar to his father as he had thought; he forgave.

But learnt to lie.

He learnt to lie about who he was, to deceive people – it worked, if people thought he was rich, he was powerful, he was straight; he was suddenly accepted. He was popular and he was loved. The occasional female fling here and there; he called it keeping up appearances. Using women?

Maybe

More than a half of the way through the week, more than half the way through the anticipatory thumps of her heart. Tonight was another of those Friday nights spent in the heart of the cosmopolitan body that was the city. The snobbery of ordering drinks priced by street name instead of content supplied Abigail with the heartily dissatisfied resignation that she had been forced to grow accustomed to.

Nobody around her knew her, yet they were all the platinum soldiers that marched around in some interconnecting regiment. Signatures here. Postage stamp there. As much as she hated the world of paperwork, of constantly sorting through the shipping orders of a stationary company; it was the best stationary company.

Abigail always wanted to be the best. She strived with an endless sense of fragility to climb ladders that she often had to manufacture herself. She didn't expect to be a sob story, but equally, was totally unqualified to know whether she was or not. Her efforts were not the sad thing; it was her belief that they were worth something that was.

She stared into the glass of red.

Who needed philosophy when red wine was around?

An appreciation of her surrounding was not something that came easily to her; rarely did the shielded need to worry about what was going on around them. Mummy and Daddy could do that for them.

But her alienation from them, since Marcus, of course, had forced a belated maturation. Suddenly all of those doors that had at once been filled with his kind-hearted bastardisations of affection were swept clear, and instead of being able to take her own tentative steps out of them, she was met at the doorstep by traffic lights, pollution, late nights in a sweaty office cubicle, typing until false nails fell off and wandering male hands in central office.

The pay was acceptable. Not good, but acceptable. Studio flat. Regular supply of new shoes. Everything that was important.

Time to leave.

She had changed out of her suit after finishing work, now wearing a sparingly cut top, jeans, low heels. As she swung her coat on, right arm first, she nudged the stool underneath the bar with her knee. Of course, the gawking eyes of the male fan club – also know as the male population – would follow her to the door. This time, though, she wouldn't give them rope to pull on. What would he think of that?

Loyalty, for a long time, was a missing component in Abigail's life. She was never given any, but had so often offered it without hesitation. Marcus cheated and the offer was retracted. It started as a weekend hobby; flashing a bit of leg at the bar, a cheeky smile, the occasional hint of cleavage.

This form of man-fishing was not only easy, but it was pitiful. They bit on every hook that she dipped into their testosterone pond.

She got what she wanted.

Now, though, she had handed in her fishing rod, and the baiting had stopped. Jack was something different. He cared, and she knew that he would never let her down. He was a real man, unlike Marcus.

The marble latticed stairs of idealism became a violently shaking escalator, moving almost too fast for Abigail to wedge a lofty heel into; but not quite fast enough. On she clung, stomach in, shoulders back, head first into the dismal pool of bittersweet letdown, and the limits of aimless goals.

Next bar. More male eyes.

As there was no longer a sobering glass of wine in front of her, she allowed her philosophical qualities to surface yet again, and half chuckled half cringed at how throughout marriage and singularity, she craved male attention and had been to extents that respectability would have to question, but since Jack, she didn't need that attention.

No more wine. She was still under the limit.

Yes, yes, yes. As if charged with the same spontaneous impulsiveness that was driving Abigail, the car's engine roared and in no time at all, and with a new found excitement, the four tyres spun hard and fast. Left turn. There was a unique buzz to be derived from the romantic notion of appearing in a bloom of romantic nostalgia.

She missed him, wanted to be with him, he had promised her he wanted the same. There was nothing but an unwritten tradition binding her to the once-a-week meetings. The stigma of their relationship holding some sort of forbidden properties was a subconscious warning device. Paranoia, Abigail told herself. Gear change

With her left hand, she fiddled with her hair, hoping that with enough flicking and twiddling it would somehow sort itself out, with her right, she lorded over the steering wheel, directing herself towards perfection.

***

The house smelt of expensive women.

Toilet cleaner, he thought. He shut the door behind him. There Jack was to greet him; perfection. Two years of perfection, in a suit, in a tie, in a white shirt. They held one another. Two men fitted together so much better than if there were two obnoxious lumps in the equation.

Sean looked around, noticing that the room had been cleaned.

What was Jack feeling guilty about?

Of course, the response was a sarcastic comment, to move conversation on. Always just to keep moving on. Charm, cashmere and conversation, Sean thought as he moved through the lounge, kicked off his trainers, watched them roll militaristically into an obtuse clatter atop one another on the peach carpet, and entered their kitchen.

Where was his birthday present?

"Turn around."

Sean followed the instructions. Jack had his hand outstretched. His proposal was simple.

Both rings were of the same steely, shiny, pure silver. The kingdom was nearly complete; two new Princes, one charming, one not.

The moon watched in his fairy state, drowsy, but not yet asleep. The little red car had made remarkable progress through the night; turning left, then right, not needing to turn back even once. That was particularly remarkable.

The speakers inside the car were pumping the air with all of the chart topping optimism that the public so adored, but the sound waves could not penetrate the bubble that Abigail had become enveloped in. Such a beautiful bubble, she thought.

There was no real room, nor need for her sometimes philosophical interjections, but instead time for the exciting possibilities that were opening up; those marble steps that she had earlier clutched at as they turned into a sadistic elevator were getting no further away, she felt. The elevator was now moving at a gradual pace. Gear change. She could drive faster than the elevator could rise, and move faster than the idealistic chasm that was threatening to undermine everything and become her death pit could open up.

The first step was this journey, out of sync, a slash in the tapestry, a change of tempo. She could be with Jack within five minutes. Left turn. She had no reason to be afraid, and felt no fear.

White wine, chicken, Chris de Burgh playing in the background, six little candles. The dinner of consolation. The air was thick, not with tension, not with discomfort, but with the sanguine weight of the future wrestling to win over the past and the present. There was, Sean thought, little competition. There was, Jack thought, little to fight for.

Abigail questioned why it was she never seemed to be able to figure out which junction to leave at. And as she was questioning this, gritted her teeth; she didn't want to burst the bubble with venomous spikes.

Nothing could go wrong, if she just stayed calm. How could anyone stay calm in a storm of inspiration though? After much deliberation, she decided that rings weren't necessary for a proposal.

Four minutes.

Sean smelt sweet, as usual. Inexpensive aftershave, regularly reapplied. The television was on, but was only being watched as justification for paying the license. Both of them could live without constant reminders of how the media ruled the world. There was still the invitation-only sense of sickness that butterflies always caused when they entered the stomach.

It was glorious, and Sean was buzzing. The television was a pest. The two could go for a walk, he suggested? Jack leant over, got close to him. Maybe not.

Right turn.

The uninvited butterflies had swarmed into the windows of the little red car, diffused through the indestructible poignancy of her love bubble, and set up camp in the top of her stomach. The chart-toppers became the silent violins, that usually only came out in movies; their discord being harmonious to Abigail's world-deaf ears. There it was. Her philosophical senses tried to stand up and make a point, but in the chaotic gathering that was her internal monologue, were drowned out along with inhibition and common sense.

How would she ask? One knee?

Two minutes

Nobody could claim that Jack didn't get value for money when he purchased his bed. It was a safe harbour, where he was the King and Queen, not just Prince Charming. His kingdom was far stretching, annexing anything that wandered into his web. It was not a matter of lying to people, he kept reminding himself.

In equal measure, the world and her ways kept reminding him that he could only get away with things for so long. He wasn't in some distant forest now; he was facing the stone cold machinations of his own existence.

The gravel crunched in a rewarding way. The tyres had finally given up their claim to control, in the same way as the rest of the car had seemed to do, and the journey went smoothly. Abigail thought she should take a few minutes to compose herself.

But preparation only killed spontaneity.

She took her first step towards the door.

Her heart was not experiencing its usual fluster of heart beats. Second step. Her feet were somewhere down there, she could see them, but she had no way of proving that they still belonged to her. Third step. What could go wrong?

She rang the doorbell.

Sean and Abigail looked at each other.

***

But the changing of emotion,
Is dead, but to the soul,
As the drilling needs of anger,
Eat away to leave a hole.

Belle was running now, she could feel the air surrounding her; hear the drums in her chest. Invigorated, more than afraid. She did not need long. There were a thousand paths ahead of her, but she didn't need to decide. The clearing called out to her, drawing her in, two old friends that met at night under the protective eye of the moon.

The three of them could not exist without one another.

Her dress was the same every time, but the bruising was different. Sometimes she had not been able to defend herself so well, and would arrive with a bloodied nose, a burst lip or with dented pride. They would never win though, they couldn't hurt her in the clearing, they couldn't even come close to hurting her.

The air was cooler there.

The place was a home to her, where she could take her cider and her cigarettes and her freedom and could be at one with herself, and face up to anything that had shaken her. Whether she would be alone there or not, was never a question.

They always found her. She could always face them there, though.

CHAPTER II

Insecurity

& Other Minds

The light-bending shade of the young woman's red hair was impressive. In the same way that light reflected off of oil paintings, there was an artistic sheen to her features; the way her nose was sculpted to guide the light to give equal attention to the collection of faint freckles running across the top of her cheeks, and her desirable complexion, along with accenting her cheek bones, which were to be admired more than noticed.

A simple ensemble; long sleeved black, roll-necked jumper, quality leather belt and dark denim bootcut jeans. The contemporary hourglass, not an extreme, but a well-kept figure. Tall, in order that her hair was not wasted, as it spanned all of her back. In the right light – which this so happened to be – Shona was more the oil painting than the person. Her tangible sobriety made the still air around her drunk, drawing in quick glances from the occasional lovestruck-but-bored boyfriend, playing in her fire, not letting the girlfriend see.

It was a terrible shame that the fire burning inside was the quintessential contrast to the fire that burned from her head. Cold. Scared. Questioning. The black dog, it had once been called.

The art gallery was something of an escape from the worries.

Her organic eyes masquerading as radiant blue marbles, as pieces of art, met with the real falsity of the painting before her. A Lady of Royal blood, she was informed by the plaque beneath the masterpiece. Shona wondered what her plaque would say, and at once developed the clammy, sick, sinking feeling that had the terrible habit of rising from her gut and teasing her neck into submission; until her throat began to grow thick. The plaque would let people know about her. They would judge her, and she wouldn't be there to tell them otherwise.

She knew the sensation better than she knew any friend. Sensation was constant, friends were not.

A sudden blast to the front of her head, the application of a smothering punch that wouldn't let go. A clothes peg to the bridge of her nose. Breathing suddenly became an Olympic sport. Hyperventilation. A hangover turned into a hanging.

Boom.

Her heart jumped, as if to try to shake off the clothes peg. The roll-neck jumper swiftly became a cage. She couldn't take it off. Sweat. She reached out with her hand, dropping her notepad in the process. Overheating. Compression. Constriction.

Boom.

People were looking. Blushing sounded too dainty, she flushed a bright red; her hair seemed to grow jealous, sticking to the sweat on her forehead in defiance, as if to try to punish her. Panic. She tried to run. Both from the panic attack and from the room. Her jeans tightened around her thighs, to match the restrictive tension that her jumper had developed. Gasping.

Tiny specks of flame abruptly took flight in front of her eyes. Fireflies. Dizzy fireflies. She felt light-headed. Gasp. She couldn't take in enough air. She felt a sharp pain run up her right hand side as she landed on it, her knees automatically wrenching up towards her. She began to pant. She felt like a dog, curled up in a fetal, useless position.

Why did she have to be so useless?

Useless, useless, useless.

The word resounded like a vile echo in her head, as she heard the blood swelling in her ears. As quickly as it whooshed around inside her, her eyes shut and she was cleared from the situation.

Useless, as always.

The savagery with which the pen dug into the paper was not a sign of the writer's despair, or anger, just a sign that the pen wasn't working. Finally, a trail of blue ink followed the fine point, impregnating the paper beneath with a concise, well-practiced signature.

Entrance into the building had never been easy. The last three months, every day, the same security guard would hand Shona the same piece of paper, the same pen, at the same time and expect the same thing to be written. Being honest with herself, she quite enjoyed the routine quality of it, but could not help but feel a degree of hurt deep down, that the little man still did not seem to acknowledge her as a person, as a professional or as a colleague until she had scribbled artfully on the dotted line. This hurt, of course, was kept buried under the hangover's smile, showing enough teeth to pass as acceptable, but not too many to seem suspicious, along with the conversation-retardant nature of the female ability to seem so entirely enraptured with one's own hair.

Good morning.

Hollow words, but accepted unquestioningly. She felt every one of the building's eyes hit her as she entered the rotating door at the same point as yesterday, and once again felt the primal need to escape fill her. Two exits were available to her, and with a well-practiced nervousness, Shona made her decision within a second and, once on the other side of the doors, set her eyes on the toilet's entrance across the way.

Yesterday, there were three hurdles to jump; today it seemed to be just the one.

Good morning.

Hollow words, accepted begrudgingly by Shona, who would much have preferred for the universal mute button to have been as depressed as she was. The toilet sign moved further away. Chitchat. Smalltalk. Bullshit. Of course, being rude wouldn't be becoming; but there was a hint of fluster setting in. Shona had not even questioned the intentions of the verbal assailant; where had the office-work converser come from? Why would she want to talk to Shona?

She had to get away.

Run away. She was sure people must be looking.

The toilet door summoned her; not a urinary calling, but a safe haven, a cubicle with a lock. Occupied, on the door. Nobody argued with a tiny lock; it could protect her. Give her time to take a swig of confidence, and re-emerge, better put together, calmer and less afraid.

The meeting hall was nearly full, seventeen seats, fifteen persons.

One entered; a beer belly with a bushy, bearded face. Thick brown hair, blistered with the grey streaks that middle age donated, free of charge. The charity was unappreciated by the barrel of a man, as one could expect. Maybe it depressed him; maybe that was why he ate so much, Shona thought as she followed him in, full of confidence. Seventeen seats, seventeen persons. Doors shut.

The morning's key speaker was the firebrand herself; as usual. It was no surprise to all members of the room that Shona had been elected as the committee member to speak. Big business deals were her specialty. Her tone never faltered. Strong, broad vowels.

It was the Irish in her.

Introduction. The key starting points rolled off of Shona's tongue, her note cards had been left in the car – all they ever did was in defiance of physics anyway: undermining the gravity of her persuasive abilities. Thirty seconds in, the time to make the kill; first impressions were out of the way – always beyond reproach, she knew that – and money could be mentioned. What her company wanted to take. The skill was in making that part totally clear, so clear in fact that it detracted from the *why* and the *what else* of the situation.

Five minutes in. The room was enveloped by her self-assured reasoning – now she was just having fun. Orating in the blurry haze that she had created for herself. The shroud was entirely compelling.

Not only did the room listen to her, but the room wanted to listen to her.

Question. Directed at her, by a deserter from her flock. Desertion was not allowed.

The man asked it with such confidence. Tried to puncture the glass balloon with a feather. He failed. Shona was once again in control. The speech drew to an end, the applause sounded, saluting her abilities. She sat down, waited for her head to catch up with her, and smiled. This was a toothy smile. The hangover from earlier had been drowned. The nervousness from earlier had been drowned.

The room was amazed at how convincing her conciseness had been. Shona was amazed at how convincing her act had been.

The room thanked her. The beer-belly thanked her.

Shona thanked the vodka.

The window had been left wide open. There was stillness in the room, though, despite the breeze strolling round. Attempts earlier in the day to dislodge some paperwork, or to upset the cat had seemingly come to an end, as the room was still papered twice; once with pastel wallpaper, once with an ever-thickening layer of documentation.

Where the aesthetics of the room were relatively sweet, the scent was unsavoury.

Shona's bedroom, office, hiding place and heartland shared the same four walls, and the same position being the second of the flat's tiny rooms. Multi-purpose was the excuse for the degradation of anything artistic within. The other room in the flat, off of the fork to the left at the reception area, belonged to abstraction; in the form of the lounge. A mess of pink leather sofas, covered in tactically placed cushions.

Cover a stain, and it's forgotten.

Shona's philosophy on household maintenance was not widely acclaimed.

Her eyes were bloodshot. Red hair, red eyes, red cheeks. Bottle in hand. Red handed. Bottle on the table. Red wine. There was a certain generosity of spirit awarded to her in her moments of sobriety: the interim between getting in from work, sitting on one of the pink leather sofas, and lifting her antidote.

The mask that her nights alone could paint on her, was so craftily manufactured by the alcohol in conversation with her brain, the soft, sinewy brain that was being carved up like an alcoholic turkey, that it made her realize that she was more than just a blocked pore on the face of some unwashed, over-greasy planet.

She bathed in the luxurious numbness that she could so easily sink into; all it took was a little help from her friends at the corner shops and her throat's ability to swallow. That easily influenced, toxic-basted turkey in her head didn't matter, anymore.

Nominal abandonment of rationality, the therapist had said.

Nominal abandonment of irrationality was her intrepid answer.

The world hated her, and she needed the simple guidance that alcohol gave to her. Her gums were stinging. Her liver was oozing with a toxicity that would have killed anybody who had any desire to live.

Stagnation of the mind, the therapist had said.

Stagnant in a stagnant pool, she remembered thinking, but could never say. The bitch that had sat opposite her was judgmental. Although she refuted respect for the sanctity of her mind, and any of her abilities, she remembered noting with the utmost conviction that the more educated one was, the less they actually seemed to know. There seemed to be nothing as powerful as real experience on forming opinions. Education gave one side of an argument, experience offered the other.

Head rush. Cheeky spirits playing games with her synapses.

Unfortunately for her; in befriending alcohol, she gave it a personality. And all great personalities were a letdown in the end. What was she doing to herself? The silence in her head was filled mostly of screaming, screeching voices. All of them with pointing fingers, accusative of walking, talking, thinking, feeling, breathing, her being wrong.

There it was. The issue.

Shona's perfect figure, ocean eyes, balmy skin were all wrong. In the eyes of the world, at least. Of that, she was certain.

Everywhere she went, people stared at her, laughing, mocking her with their better ways. Her head was a war zone, between the knowledge that she might do something wrong, and the fear that she might be laughed at without knowing it.

It wasn't that she hated herself; it was that she hated the fact she didn't know if everyone else did. She was a lone, red beacon in the dead centre of a frozen pond, trying to find her feet, but just ending up chilled by the lack of stability. What were people thinking?

She wished she could slice open peoples heads, pull out their thoughts, copy them, paste them, save them, back them up.

The insecurity that she had nurtured rose up against its tiny mother, took advantage of her, played with her and made her question herself. The insecurity was the Judas child that had grown up as overconfidence, and suddenly mutated with the jibes of others.

Was she too fat?

Was she too thin?

Was her hair too red?

Was she wearing the right thing?

Were people looking at her chest?

The Judas gene became a parasitic paranoia when Shona was a teenager. Comments accumulated, but were outwardly taken on the chin. She would just laugh it off, to move on conversation. Always just to keep moving on.

Timidity. Shona reverted into herself; insecurity took control of her confidence.

Introversion. Shona's inner voice became louder than her outer.

Except of course when she hid inside a bottle, wrapped up warm in the teddy-bear grip of alcohol. It could continue for a short time, years maybe, but it was a safety net that she needed – anything, to guide her out of her shell, before Judas tugged on the reigns, and wrenched her back inside. Even the knowledge that one day that teddy-bear would grow up in to a big, bleeding, weeping, angry, cancerous deterioration of her insides didn't deter her – she knew she couldn't win. Shona thought back to the art gallery. The plaque, beneath the portrait of her life. She had been a good person to those around her, but how could she be sure that would be remembered? That they would return her affections?

She couldn't.

Choke. She spluttered some of her acidic remedy out, pangs of panic niggling at her corners, threatening to rip her up again. What would people remember her for? Would they think about her fondly? Or would they still hate her?

Would Judas really be that unkind; and let her have yet another breakdown?

Of course.

Her insecurities about what the world thought of her once again struck fickle victory, having forced their way from her stomach, up through her throat and into a jumble of vomit and blood on her once clean carpet.

Lub-dub. Heartbeat.

Lub-dub. Heartbeat.

The window had spent another night left open. Shona has spent another night spread out on a burgundy rug. As she stirred, earlier than usual, she momentarily felt embarrassment that she had had the audacity to buy a rug the colour of wine, in the knowledge that it would need to be capable of offering stains a safe harbour. Cover a stain, and it's forgotten.

The sun had not quite clambered to his height. Shona didn't have to be in work today - probably why she had managed to wake up on time without an alarm.

Lub-dub. She rolled over onto her side. Her hand was wet with the same sick as her foot. She was no better at aiming down than out, she thought with a bashful rage, as she noticed the small territory of semi-digested food acting as a campsite for several gypsy flies.

Lub-dub. She rose with a languid rigidity, avoiding the sick-pasted arm coming into contact with anything else. The black top came off. The wind breathed in through her window, and ticked the thin, faint hairs on the top of her back and neck. Jeans next, then bra. She sauntered slowly through the cesspit, into the bathroom.

Shower on, knickers off.

She sighed underneath the disheartening warmth of the water. Her head ached, and her eyes stung, and the motion of applying shampoo was making her feel sicker than she had felt previously. The sun reached his morning height.

Good morning.

Hollow light seeping into a hellish cage.

Frustration was born. The weight pushing down on Shona's bare shoulders slid down to caress her back, before grabbing her at the sides, pushing in, drilling blunt fingernails between each rib, creating a pressure. Adrenalin. *Lub-dub*. As she stepped out of the shower, she overestimated the ability of her hangover-flooded head to keep up, and felt it catch up with her, slamming back into place with a dull thud.

Her bedroom, office, hiding place and heartland was the resting place of one of the two unclosed windows – they could not be described as open, any more than Shona could. Feeling ridiculous about everything, from the word go until now, she stood naked and looked down at the occasional pedestrian wandering around.

An old man, his grandson, his grandson's friend. Three heads, all filled with different thoughts, occasionally about the same thing, hopefully never about her. She ran a hand through her hair, arctic spittle was flicked out onto her soft, pale back. The massiveness of her aptitude for failing in existence formed a bluebell around her, and the forest of her mind swallowed her up. With a bare leg, she kicked out. The wine rack fell.

Shona was alone and sober and still.

Still afraid

***

In a cloud of lustful mercy,
A busy calm, one can find,
The midnight jealousy,
Of a dreamer's mind.

Belle could hear them coming, their footfalls rapidly approaching now. There were endless ways to get to the clearing, but only she could leave again; that was the crutch that supported her. The youthful confidence that she was a liberty to administer was a refreshing, rainless storm. Where were they?

They were lost, she bet with herself. The problem was not that they could outsmart her, no, they were quite stupid, in fact. The problem was that they were inevitable. They were freeloading bastards with a goal to attain – their means were never judged, only ever considered unfortunate. Their demonic properties seemed laughable, as the pitter-patter of incoherent, out-of-place feet stumbled in persuit of their prey. She was asking them to dance. Inviting them to waltz – but on her terms, to her tune. There lay was the threat.

The very rare threat.

Soon, she could see them, touch them, smell them and let them see her, and how they repulsed her. The squares were gone, and the chess pieces had been set loose.

Belle smiled. She was in power.

For now.

Loneliness & Crowds

Dostoyevsky was a great man. Max turned the final page of the breezeblock-sized novel, and felt a mixture of melancholy and relief. Relief, firstly at the traditionally poignant non-resolution, and secondly that in finishing the book, came the promise that the breeze-block would no longer have to be hauled onto and off of buses every day.

The early morning hours had come in fast, an unnoticed tide to a bookworm. His bedside lamp had grown warm, as had the cogs of his mind, as he lay there, aware of the passage of time but not what it signified, mulling over ideas presented to him in fine craft.

His pregnant intellect, though, could not sustain his body any more than physical exuberance could sustain his mind. As the well-oiled workings of his brain were invigorated in the same way as a recently scattered field, his eyelids dropped, cutting off mind from matter.

Tall, thin, pale, sandy haired, youthful looking.

Tucked up in white sheets. The lamp had been left on; the reflection in the mirror was that of an ethereally illuminated figure, placed gently among linen in body, and placed gently among calm dreams in spirit.

The truth of the matter was that his mind was not wandering the cloud-lined pathways that were expected, but instead walking along sturdy iron beams, a million miles up, suspended by no ropes; only in terror. The distant view was just a clearing. A clearing of city brick, burned by a heartless force of the unconscious, metal structures melded into one another, reaching up towards him in sordid shapes.

His balancing act came to an end, as a brazen wind overbalanced him. His tiny proportions offered him no support. He stumbled, trying with every part of his body to grab onto something, but at every contact point, the iron beam that he was standing on produced a slick, oily discharge, and stopped him from making a lasting impression.

Falling.

The wind was in his hair. Going up his nostrils. Burning cold, hitting the back of his throat as he screamed. Faster. The battering wind forced one arm to be wrenched over his back, in a newfound broken looseness, causing him to spin violently, and miss several of the metal spikes. Still falling at dizzying speeds, with heightening turning momentum, he felt ice cold air hack behind his eyeballs. The atmosphere's blunt, rusty razor blades were forcing their way into his head. He wasn't even breathing any more.

Gasping. Falling. Writhing. Agony.

A red curtain began to close inside his head; the capillaries inside the fragile little skull popping like unheard fireworks. He felt each one of the thousand inflame into globular blood tears, which were quickly left behind as his meteoric plunge continued. Max's sight became estranged, but still in blindness he was plummeting. He was left to cry through broken eyes.

He had lost one of his senses in a senseless scenario.

Irony didn't save him. Crunch.

Slowly, with a submissive composure Max's moist eyes opened, the warm lamp still giving light to the broken angel on the bed. His wings were as absent from the sepia scene of the early morning as they had been in his sleeping mind, and every day of his life.

Now as awake as he ever was, there was a spring missing from his step that was just as absent from the air. April was meant to be a spring month, yet seemed to be teasing people, convincing them that there would be a sudden emergence of heat - then as soon as they left their houses, audaciously pointing at their lack of that extra winter layer and laughing at it with a polar breath.

Max was always cold, though, so managed to get the better of spring's childish pranks. The pavement beneath him met feet inside socks, inside another pair of socks, and thick boots. Combats, boxers, t-shirt, shirt.

Warm enough for a poor winter, warm enough for a rich spring.

Someone he knew. Smile. No small talk.

His walking was rhythmic, just a means of getting to a destination. One, two, one two. Cross the road. He didn't feel the need to look left and right; if anything happened, the driver would get the blame anyway. Pavement. Keep walking. His eyes kept watching the floor in front of him. As he continued his solemn march, he wondered if anybody else could see the black cloud above his head, it's nighttime furore bellowing into his ears, thunderclaps of maniacal hands.

His face felt featureless as it was licked by the winter side of the weather's schizophrenic tongue. He looked up to the sign of the bookshop. Engraved in an ancient wood, from some faraway forest.

Almost a smile.

Max's gut began to swarm, as it did every day. Symbolic not of bad seafood, but of the tornado of tiny butterflies that had begun to spin hysterically inside. Momentarily, his black cloud gave way to a ray of scorching light. In a sensual lucidity, he lifted his head up, reuniting with all the other clouds, and he felt a certain twang of exhilaration. It would almost be a shame if today were the day that he finally had the balls to do it. *Almost*.

He honestly did not know if he would.

Hand on door handle. Enter. Ding-a-ling; entrance bell. Nobody looked up. He remained painfully anonymous, despite his having ding-a-linged every day for the past three weeks, at a similar time. The counter staff had changed configuration, as they seemed to do on every one of his appearances. Anonymity in hand, he continued his progression through the shop, filling yesterday's footprints, he thought.

Stairs. Since the cloud had sluggishly manoeuvred back into position atop his fair hair, he had been weighed down by the heavyweight shadow being cast upon him. His mission was clear, but such repetitive, aggressive failure in the past had caused him to lose faith in his abilities.

Maybe today was the day.

First floor. The effort of the stairs would have hurt more if the butterflies hadn't been inside to take the blow for him. It had been suggested that the problem with heightened intellect, was heightened imagination, and heightened sensual appreciation. That might explain the precipice that Max now stood on tiptoes at the edge of.

He had fallen every day for the last twenty days. Straight into unforgiving hands that promised, without fail, to punch into his core, turning bone to pulp, and squeeze his heart, causing it to shrivel and warp.

Left foot. He stepped forward, finding the wooden floor beneath him a silent stage for his trepidation. His right foot followed like an unwilling child, being forced by the feverish parent that was Max's fading will to succeed.

He hadn't fallen yet.

The upstairs payment counter arrived. Where was she? Where the hell was she? Making momentary eye contact with the empty eyes of the short, the fat, the ugly, he scanned the storage area behind the counter.

He was overbalancing.

Wait.

There she was.

Perfection in a five-foot-two package. The butterflies exploded, his internal systems brimming into a mass of petal-wings. He ignited. The black cloud was absorbed by the radiance of his lustful courage.

He stood strong.

For the twenty-first time in twenty-one days he swam in Petrarchan waters.

Ten seconds passed.

For the twenty-first time in twenty-one days; he drowned.

Bookshop-girl.

That was the identifier. He was Max and she was Bookshop-girl. Any kind of conversation always went out of the window when infatuation swooped down and flapped up in his face, scratching his tenderness with spiteful wings – hence, he had never managed to find out anything about her. Not even her name.

Pathetic; one of the few thoughts that were constantly there in the back of his head, swarming around the locked doors of the mental shrine that he had created in honour of her. His frailty was constantly a surprise to him, yet its existence still caused him anguish – an emotion that he thought would have retired after year-after-year of teenage exercise.

Top floor studio flat. Shoebox.

He didn't bother with radiators; they would only warm up his skin. Warm skin wouldn't make anything any better; unless, of course, it was Bookshop-girl's warm skin, and he was allowed to be near it without a counter and a black cloud in between. He didn't need his flat to be warm, anyway, there was enough condensation going on already. Too much of anything was bad for you.

He wanted someone to talk to.

He could go downstairs, find someone; there had to be some company for him in the building. The woman with the little red car on the ground floor, or the redhead on the floor above? They seemed pretty normal to him. That was what he needed; the company of untroubled people.

The idea was fleeting. Loneliness in its most uncompromising form was repellent to vanilla company, it needed cracking with the perseverance that could only be born from intimacy. In any form.

His hands were steady, his face was not marred with abuse and his ego still formed a failing balloon above him enough to keep him afloat in the superficial mud puddle that the species seem to luxuriate in. Pigs in shit. And they were in deep.

It was not his hands or face or the traditionally male defensive ego that was failing. None of them hurt. None of them were sinking with titanic depreciation. Max's insides were, however, being ceaselessly flooded by solitary waves. Three, hour-long minutes passed. He had not moved. What was the point?

He swallowed. His mouth had dried up like his inspiration. There was one place he could go to chase the lost cause. He opened a book and joined his only friends.

Voices were a disturbing luxury, but always present in department stores. Max was no social commentator, and didn't really give a damn what people did with their lives, nor what they thought of him in return, but he couldn't help but notice that the commercialisation of the shopping climate was not only brutal, but it was cheerless and as artificial as his shell.

A false smile from the mannequin behind the counter. A false smile returned. Stuck-on, plastic nails handed over a plastic bag, paid for by a plastic card. No organic interaction, and no chance of organic intimacy. At least books were made from tree's paper he thought; something with origins in the unprocessed world.

People flocked, following their herd instincts from shop to shop, pushing, barging each other out of the way. They were all just maggots there, wriggling around; some trying too hard to blend into the background, others trying too hard to stand out. Daylight was ostensibly unfashionable, being replaced by the electric medium.

Max slithered through the crowd, his cloud following him loyally.

He bought enough that he wouldn't need to move in such fabricated circles for a while – why was it that everything *he* felt was painfully, profoundly, acutely real? Any and all appearances were just as bad. He was alone with those who had been crafted in literature, the only people who could truly sympathise, who knew the pain of being alone in a crowded room.

He stood alone, among the many. He was not a martyr to any cause, nothing so noble, but a slave to an infatuated isolation. He lacked courage, yet not conviction, a paradox that was ripping him apart, unpicking his stitches with the same blunt blades that attacked him at night as he slept.

There was a temperance of spirit about him that seemed more tainted than were he to exude the collective instincts of the hive that he was born a part of. His shores were contaminated with vacuum-packed solidarity, and he was forever shackled to them; voices left foreign ports and were met by the poetic injustice that should, he begged, be confined solely to novels.

With his ever growing lacklustre, he continued to burrow into the crowd, trying to lose his cloud, and fill the desperate cavity inside his ribcage with anything but the filthy sensation that fizzed and buzzed perpetually.

Max had been so close to beauty. But, as he gave up inhibition to make a grab at it, in its infinite glory, he was swatted like a fly by infatuation; which took the place of love in the equation. Displacement, a scientist would have said.

His instincts told him to keep breathing. Animal instincts.

His steps on day twenty-two were different. Spring steps.

In the full knowledge that he had the unearthly climb to the top of the stairs, with a sudden burst of frustration, Max ran.

Across the road without looking, up onto the pavement, head up this time, step after step – *don't step on the cracks, it's bad luck* – he was pissed off, and bored of being pathetic.

Nearly there. Determination drove the human machine now, ignoring the adverse weather conditions; black clouds were no bother. Determination, though, if unsupported, deflates as sourly as the male ego. Max couldn't do it. He had to try. Determination gave one final push, then died like the temporary impulse that it was.

Ding-a-ling. No response – none expected.

There they were, the first hurdle in the race; the stairs. The kinetic properties of determination were failing, but had inspired a momentary inflammation of Max's senses. His ascent was casual. As he was met with the mental precipice, the kinetics drove on, not looking back as they were engulfed by the fear of the fall.

With a sense of queasy déjà vu, Max marched on, the twenty-second hatch of butterflies had descended upon him as was expected, and were maturing with every step. There must have been a hole in his black cloud, as there was room enough for the taunting eyes of fate to glare through with monstrously dilated pupils and a grotesquely malformed sense of humour .

Bookshop-girl was there, as was expected, but next to her was fate's foul minion. Shorter than Max, taller than her, fair haired, tanned, despicably charming. Fate hadn't had enough – and dealt a second hand. For the first time in twenty-two year-long days, Bookshop-girl spoke. Could she help Max?

No. Thank you.

Dual pressures pierced his externality, the first a direct result of the repulsion he was filled with on seeing fate's bastard, the second the sheer excitement of being spoken to by beauty; which under the circumstances was incongruously brutal.

He felt sick. Physically nauseated.

She was meant to be his. His alone, to be claimed when he could.

Pathetic; one of the few thoughts that constantly bombarded the once holy shrine that Max had built in the back of his mind in honour of his fallen god, as he raced a snail home and lost.

There was a new light in his flat.

Burning books in the sink.

One of the two things he loved had been stolen from him, now he was sacrificing the other. Surely there was some compassion in the universe? It was just a matter of finding it. Max threw another volume of friendship on the fire, and watched his comrades burn.

The heat given off offended him.

How dare he gain anything of use from the loss of his crutches?

Maybe he couldn't, he admitted, as he broke in half, crashing to the floor, wrapping his arms around his legs, searching for foetal comfort. There was none to be found.

There was no sign of the rationality of thought that was considered necessary in a personal crisis, that was often offered by those closest to the failing component. Who would rescue a sinking island? Friends were such an impermanent feature in Max's tapestry, coming and going, seemingly when it suited them. His secrecy had nothing to do with it, his mantra dictated.

There was the resolute circle of long-lasting acquaintances, who masqueraded as self-titled friends, who took it upon themselves to enter into his life and push him out. They were there to *support him,* he mulled with a sense of incredulity.

Where were they now?

Where had the promises gone?

He knew. They were with the flavour of the month, or so absorbed in their self-adoring fetishes that they had rewritten their list of priorities, and not told him. Fate and friendship had moved the goalposts, and left him standing in the middle of a sodden field, sending him helplessly down into the ground.

As the black cloud sunk on his horizons forming a solid black tunnel, he thought for a fleeting second that he saw the silvery light of hope in the crowded periphery. As the light rushed off to take its place at the end of the tunnel, Max snatched at it with several handfuls of painkillers.

Max sat bookless and alone in the lamplight.

His wings were still broken.

***

The clearing of the fog,
In the clearing of the mind,
Is a hidden truth,
Meant not for mankind.

Belle was surrounded, her red dress twirling with her as her ears picked up the others' proximity. They were gargantuan, and disgusting. They knew what she was thinking – to her shame, they often controlled what she was thinking.

But not now. Not here.

The first appeared in a cloud of unfaithful dishonesty, his prey arriving with him.

Belle felt her nature become all too familiarly human; and compassion set in. The urge to let the suited cloud swallow her up again was almost irresistible. His thrall was entrancing, and raw, and magnetic. His suit was, as always, immaculate.

But not now. Not here.

More movement. She spun. Her dress followed. The second of them appeared.

Different to the first, but just as destructive, and a product of different venom. Belle clenched her jaw, and faced glazed over, blue eyes straight on. Putting a face to a name was a powerful tool. Belle wondered what the blue eyes were thinking, were they judging?

A third arrival.

A pathetic morsel, the result of desertion. But Belle felt for this one; the maximum amount of support that she could feel for any of them. This one was empty and lonesome. In any other place, she would let his black cloud overshadow her.

But not here. Not now.

The clearing was nearly a full house.

One more approached, slower to develop than the rest, yet just as capable of destruction. Four great issues would soon be brought together, all with eyes to look into and all with faces to admire.

Belle was being faced with humanity.

CHAPTER IV

Self-Loathing
& Oneself

It may not have been the Bard, but some overeducated thinker somewhere along the line had dedicated their life to the construction of the theory that *a life without drama was a life without living.*

Tragedy was Shakespeare's domain, and a bitter medicine that Sandra felt no compulsion to remedy herself with. The distinct lack of tragedy, any drama of any description, secreted from her in sweaty patches; soaked up by her white blouse, clearly visible to all but the blind. She was acutely aware of the hot dampness on her lower back, pasting the wisps of black hair down with surprising adhesive success. The sticky back patch was not on public display, but the underarm swamps were.

In her beastly state, she trotted lethargically towards the tower of books that had been watching her eat her openly broadcast second breakfast. There was no sand around, so she buried her head in paper instead. If anybody spoke to her, of course they would be greeted with the jovial exuberance that she had forced them to grow accustomed to through her constant bombardments of soprano squeaks of glee at something pink, or something fluffy.

Her façade no more convinced anybody else than it did her, but in believing that she was *considered* happy, irony allowed her to suction out some self-respect. *Some*. The workplace, the bookshop, the temple of tragedy; the stage for her great act.

Business was quiet. No customers to occupy her wandering mind. She sat down, feeling her stomach land on her thighs, which in turn slapped the wooden stool. *Suck it in*. Her stomach tensed, and she sat up straight. Hopefully nobody noticed.

What if they did?

Momentary concern.

Chocolate.

No, it was not an attempt to fuel the stereotype; being overweight was a problem that she knew she had, and knew she had to face. Tomorrow. Not the same *tomorrow* that she had been talking about yesterday, though. The next one.

She was massive. *Disgusting*.

She was revolting. *Disgusting*.

Thankfully, her nemesis had stayed out of the room. There were still mirrors at home, though. Maybe that was why she so enjoyed the bookshop; having to return home to be greeted by the cold top floor of a block of flats, the universal cabbage smell, an aging door, a squeaky lock and to find all of her mirrors painted with pictures of what she hated most.

A draft of air from the ground floor signaled the arrival of a potential customer and a definite distraction. Quickly the young man climbed the diminutive flight of stairs, looking quite calm as he sauntered across the floor. *It was him* Her heart leapt slightly, and Sandra was suddenly aware of her belly overhanging flabbily, visible in the air, just a target for eye-darts. She had noticed the handsome visitor coming in at about the same time for the last couple of weeks; nobody else seemed to care.

As her considerable buttocks peeled off of the stool, her underwear performed its habitual traffic, fitting with maximum discomfort between the sagging skin pillows. She could hardly start rearranging now. *Why did this always happen?*

No time for triviality, time for courage. With an out of character step, Sandra stretched a bingo-wing up in the vain hope of making contact with some form of self-confidence. The handsome customer did not respond to her attempts at a friendly look of interest. He was probably seeing her how she did. The short, the fat, the ugly.

Self-loathing was once again inspired by loneliness.

It was a disgustingly pleasurable pain. Sandra's fingers were on a mission. She plunged them back inside; deeper this time.

They touched the top of her throat, her nails tickling the roof of her mouth, which salivated with an anxious knowledge of what was to come.

With a tightening akin to that of an electric shock, her stomach tensed up with less aesthetic merit than earlier on in the shop. Three times a day; once in the morning before work, once on her return home and then once before going to bed. Her ribs felt the familiar retrenchment of room around them, as the contents of her stomach burst forth and made an impromptu appearance, in the gloriously vile form of putrid liquid and ever-noticeable carrot slices.

Tighten. Gush.

More spewed forth in self-titled relief. Vomit was a good friend, whom she was always pleased to see.

Sandra winced in a form of distorted happiness. *Goodbye, gut*, was her defunct midnight prayer, said over the dazzling white of the toilet bowl.

Candidly speaking, experience and common sense told her that she was my no means in the bracket of healthy, or even in the ever-tightening bracket of stability. Mentally speaking, she told her self that she was fine. *Of course she was.* There was nothing wrong. *Of course there wasn't.* She had nothing to worry about. *Never.*

Prayers to the god of semi-digested food and elasticity-of-the-throat over, she stood again, fatigued and refreshed in the same thorny breath. Her skin hoped to have been forgotten about; but luck wasn't in. *No hair. No hair. No hair.* Wax on a daily basis, residual rawness covered from the bookshop's dramatic eyes by her sweat-absorbing blouses.

Why was she so disgusting?

It pained her to look into the smeared mirrors that practically tiled her flat, and see an accumulation of years of set-backs and the secret scars that tattooed her body, each representing the loss of another aimless dream.

What she didn't see, though, was the goldfish bowl that she was persistently swimming in.

The morning walk to work was pleasantly unmarred by the sceptical bleats of her stomach which regularly flocked to meet her ears at the same time as the occasional viscous messengers from her stomach acid formed a broth in her gut and introduced themselves to her tongue in a hiccup, before being swallowed back into impermanence.

Sandra had worked since she was sixteen, always being the loose cannon of the litter, deciding against any refinement an institution could offer her. She hadn't done badly out of it. Stable job, stable flat, stable routine.

Routine, routine, routine.

She arrived and looked up at the panelled exterior. The bookshop was a great place. In times of any discomfort, she seemed to draw a sense of solace from the stillness that settling dust brought about. Second hand books were the heart of an empire built on selling dreams. One day, with one box of decrepit literary outcasts, she might find a dream worth buying and keeping.

Dreams were the building blocks for everything, she pondered sentimentally, as she trudged into the bookshop. A new box awaited her unpacking abilities.

What abilities?

As she sat, her ripples of hate gave an energetic lollop before rejoining her regularly rhythmic cutting, sticking and note-making. Fulfilment was a drink best served warm and Sandra was sucking on an ice cube.

Customer; smile. Offer assistance. Fiddle in self-doubt over yet another matter. Find the answer, and give it away on a soulless plate. As Sandra gave away another serving of her utility to the consumer, she was herself consumed with the pangs of an intricate emotional malfunction, the response being that her lips dried up into a bottom-one-first trembling, and her eyes filled with an all too frequent visitor.

Idiot.

Berated by the lashes of embarrassment's public whip, she felt the eyes of the two shamefully happy lovers also behind the counter swiftly initiate every protocol that they could administer in order to avoid noticing her. In all frankness, they couldn't beat her up in the way she could herself. And planned to. *Why was she such an idiot?*

The tissue piggybacked the salty water from her cheeks, gripping hold of the water with a tight particle fist.

What was there to cry about? the riposte of *What wasn't there to cry about?* flashed into her mind with a vengeful spite, her personality beginning to lay into itself. There was no mania, just a burning hatred. Of that she was sure.

Sure, sure, sure.

Lock it and bolt it and shut the bastards out.

That was the idea.

There was an enemy on the inside, and it had to be found, and eliminated.

Or, Sandra admitted, just appeased again.

There was no time to get more naked, no time to get uglier; only enough time to stomp through from the entrance of her flat to the kitchen, to reflect with exhilaration at the compliment of cheap chocolate boxes that were stacked militaristically, and to lurch over the sink. The toilet bowl would be jealous.

As she continued with her relentless daily self-destruction, it appeared to her that there would never be a resolution. The rut was, in typically poetic fashion, endless and she was, in typically human fashion, stuck in it. *Was that an issue?*. She was fine. *Fine.*

As she wiped the last venomous drips from her lips, she stepped through the light-headedness and into her living room. A mirror grabbed her by the heart and forced her to, yet again, address it, salute it, pay homage to it – be a good slave to it.

The importance of image was not something that she could escape; of course it was the first and foremost priority. *Everybody cares.* Nobody particularly cared. The importance of personality was not something that she could embrace; something she had never been allowed to develop. The importance of a complete package, *warts and all*, was the contrary pole, and the reverse point. *Looks were everything.*

Irony, in her sardonic manner, was ubiquitous.

The decision was made. The vice had to go. *Goodbye chocolate.* Perfection was attainable. *No pain, no gain.* Were her body able to give a rational voice in protest of the notion, and persuade her that pain clearly was not the right path in this case; maybe there would be some hope. Sandra's voice, however, was under the control of one of the faulty systems.

With an unheard sigh of deprivation, her body accepted another defeat.

Sandra was the most disjointed of any character in any book she had read.

Her paragraphs were all over the place, and her story was difficult to tell. Her hand was tired; but coped with the stresses of taking dictations from her mind, as a dig at computerisation, and a dig at the sanctity of literature's blessed path into the world. A new paragraph continued her tale of resentment.

Her parents were perfect. They had formed the perfect family cocoon around her, and through nursery rhyme and romantic notions, forged a new umbilical chord for her, feeding her with the sweet nutrients of life, leaving the sour toxins outside in the cold.

It was, she thought, a shame that the cocoon had burst so belatedly, as what emerged was not the plume of silvery wings that fluttered like silk on a breeze, but instead a furry, grey moth. All teeth and anger and insipid monotony. As with many moths, before she could sink her parasitic teeth into the fabric of anything, she was swatted down by the ingenuity of society's crushing hand.

Her struggle with failure had begun at the launch of adolescence, as she was suddenly illuminated to the fact that rules were boundaries. Moth to a flame, indeed. The thrall of rule-breaking was breaking the back of the spineless constriction that she had to suffer on a daily basis. From the point of illumination, she was faced with a fork in her metaphorical path.

Her writing slowed as she began to feel a lump solidify in her throat. *It wasn't her fault.*

Lucidity was fleeting.

Writing continued.

Sandra's choice was, in itself, not unbiased. It seemed to her that in her mid-teens, on the threshold of acceptance into a repetitive and closed society, there was only one evaluation to be made; did she want to judge herself or be judged by others?

Unlike many, she was uninhibited by the choking fear of public eyes, and instead chose to be her own odious critic. As that side of the fork was chosen, she proudly boarded the train and was delivered to a state of uninterrupted instability. The public need never know, nor have a part to play in moulding the dead clay. She was her own worst enemy.

Her thoughts grew more confused, as her blood became emptier and her prime directive became all that supported her. Self-hatred was a creature of simple evil; the simplicity of cancerous multiplication – one idea led to another, then another, then another. Tunnels all had endings, but that didn't guarantee the quality of the destination, as so many had wanted her to believe as a child.

What is there to look forward to?

Paying the ferryman was the one final soulless plate that she would have to give away, and she was at the point where she didn't care when the bailiffs came. She had been running away from her own thoughts for too long, substituting their destructive effects with physical manifestations.

Starve the body to save to soul or starve the soul to save the body.

Another philosophy so open to deep thought that drowning was always the likely outcome.

Sandra's head was purged with questions that she not only considered too big for her to handle, but with home truths that she considered too inedible to accept.

Confusion. Panic. Self-inflicted uncertainty.

Irreversible uncertainty.

The sound of melancholy music drifting through the air acted as a reminder as to why she sat as a model for a devious painter, giving him her time to plot the finishing touches on the portrait of her existence. In fits of frustration and claustrophobia she complained at the tedium of day-to-day existence, forever feeling the need to selflessly punish herself for unknown crimes that she had never committed.

Tightly structured paragraph followed well punctuated verse as she tried with ever diminishing breaths to put her soul on paper. *Life matters,* she thought, as she touched yet another nerve with cat-like acuity, scribbling down depictions of her downhearted normality.

Maybe that was the problem?

Her scribbling turned to rambling, and her mania turned to pain. Her head was a battlefield, and her comedown was evidently imminent. *Fine, fine, fine* was the ongoing triplet for that hour.

For a young woman, Sandra had felt old for so long, as if her childhood had been robbed by faceless thieves that preyed on her own lack of confidence. Her ability to provide the world with a seamless façade was only ever interrupted by alcohol, and other substitutes for reality. An adoration of the real world was met with the boundlessly painful fact that she found it so hard to keep herself a part of it. People were easy, *they would believe anything*.

Now, in a last ditch attempt to outrun the self-pressured plight, that her existence had been respectful of for so long, her thoughts packaged themselves, and made the electric pilgrimage from her brain, to her hand, through a pen before arriving, tarnished, broken and disgracefully on sheets of white paper.

Occasionally, she would break from her autobiographical task to take count of the events as they actually happened, comparing them with the falsity of her words. Only *she* had to read them, and her memories had better be good.

Only after days of uncounted number, were the words finished in readiness for the slap that she knew existence would give her for undermining its authority. Her stomach was crying with gentle leaks of blood and the need for nourishment was a constant. Although her stamina was impressive, pain and reality pushed through and won unconditionally.

Her breathing became as faint as the writing from her inkless pen. Listlessly, she stood, and moved nearer an open window. Her breakdown was not slow and it was not forgiving. *She didn't deserve forgiveness*.

The regicidal Queen took her position by the window as she thought of Shakespeare again. The pen dropped out of her hand, and she was denied the last line in her verse. There was a succinct stop to her agony as her self-hatred blossomed with bloody hands and she moved down to a forced stoop. Nobody else was involved in her comedown, but herself; and that hurt most of all.

As the hospital lights overhead grew brighter, Sandra knew she would have to face the music in the form of the violins that so often accompanied tragedy.

***

The clearing of the fog,
In the forest of the mind,
Will give a stable place,
In which to face up to and to bind,
Endless human failure.

And then, before Belle, stood her five greatest weaknesses. The five causes of failure.

Lies.

Idealism.

Insecurity.

Loneliness.

Self-loathing.

They had all taken their position, in the forest of her mind. Human failure, given human faces.

Finale

For Belle, it had been a Thursday like every other.

It had been another Thursday for humanity too, exactly like every other day.

The grease that had accumulated in her hair was warm with sweat at the parting point of the pale strands of lifeless straw; nobody had the compassion to turn the heating down, and nobody had the sense, or rationality to really notice whether she was too hot or not.

She was tired, there were invisible needles probing into her head, through the corners of her eyes, trying as hard as they could to rip open her skull, to release the pressure behind her nose, in her sinuses and the sharp pains were spanning out like cancerous cells, creating a decaying sense of rot towards the back of her head and neck.

The humidity in the room was oppressive and closing in on her like slowly tightening cling-film.

The moist, fleshy skin on her left arm tingled, as its right-handed twin moved across it, in an attempt to retain some form of comfort. The claustrophobic robe of heat that she was being unwillingly swathed in made her feel out of sync with her surroundings; she was dizzy, trying to breath.

Nobody cared, of course, or she might have complained.

Nobody ever cared.

Who would care about the ramblings of an old woman, lying in a hospice bed, waiting to be struck off a list, waiting to be less of a burden to everyone? Waiting for something better.

She would be fed the lines about nightmares not being real. But they were real to her. Of course they were real; they were as real to her that night as they had been every night of her life. Of course they were real; there was nothing more real than lies, and the fear of being the human insect being crushed by one, the insecurity and the unreserved terror of what the rest of the goldfish in the bowl thought. The loneliness: the deadly void that fills the chest, and pumps it with cold, icy heat. The self loathing that fills the gut with acid, turns the stomach to wretch, and the face away from the mirror.

Back to the clearing, to the night, to the six lonely figures standing around her. She would be wearing her red dress again, be feeling the buzz of the cider again, and would be able to bathe in the wonder of her sheer courage. She could be young, and free, and angry again. And she could fight for her life, fight against everything that plagued her.

Belle could meet with her inner fears, give them a face; give them a story of their own. Yes, in that clearing she stood at least some chance of tackling them.

The demons of her mind and the fear that sat at the depths of the soul, the demons that permeated to the surface in moments of darkness, in the most self-intimate moments, when a crowd is just the wrapping on an empty box, and when voices move around, like choking, smothering lashes from callous, unseeing husks with unseen whips, were still constant whilst she was awake. But she could escape again to the clearing, and to the forest of her mind.

Every issue there was real, but wearing a coat of dense fiction.

Now though, she had to fight a new enemy. She might be young in the clearing, and brave, and the hero, but Belle had to face the resignation that she had wasted too long being bound to that dream. Instead of taking action, she had done nothing.

In reality, she had never defeated Jack's lies to Abigail, never shaken off Abigail's naïve idealism, she never lost Shona's insecurity about what others thought of her. She never lost Max's loneliness and she never lost Sandra's self-hatred – now, time had caught up with her and she had lost her chance to make the dream a reality.

Humanity's worst qualities would outlive her. Life had aged her, taken the beauty away from her face. The importance of facing up to real-life fears had become painfully clear to her.

Failure.

Belle was afraid. As usual.

It was a cliché, she knew that.

- THE END -

The Author

Sam O'Doherty